ENZO
AND THE CHRISTMAS TREE HUNT!

Garth Stein

Illustrated by R. W. Alley

HARPER

An Imprint of HarperCollinsPublishers

Library of Congress Cataloging-in-Publication Data

Stein, Garth.
  Enzo and the Christmas tree hunt! / Garth Stein ; illustrated by R. W. Alley. — First edition.
    pages cm
  Summary: Daddy, Zoe, and their dog Enzo search for the perfect Christmas tree, but when Zoe loses her
way, she learns that her family is never far behind.
  ISBN 978-0-06-229532-3 (hardback)
  [1. Dogs—Fiction. 2. Christmas trees—Fiction. 3. Christmas—Fiction. 4. Lost children—Fiction.] I. Alley,
R. W., 1955- illustrator. II. Title.
PZ7.S82En 2015   2015005623
[E]—dc23   CIP
                                                                                                                          AC

The artist used pen and ink, pencil, watercolor, gouache, acrylics,
and coffee spills on paper to create the illustrations for this book.
Typography by Rachel Zegar
15 16 17 18 19 PC 10 9 8 7 6 5 4 3 2 1
❖
First Edition

For Edgar "Eddie" Beagle
—G.S.

To Clarks Christmas Tree Farm
and our many happy holiday
family memories there
—R.W.A. and Z.B.A.

It seems like we've just finished eating the Thanksgiving turkey when Zoë starts talking excitedly about the *next* holiday.

"Christmas is the *best*!" she tells me. "First we go to the farm to find the perfect tree. Then we put it in our house and decorate it with the ornaments. And *then*, on Christmas Eve, Santa comes and covers the *whole floor* of the living room with toys!"

I don't understand why we would put a tree in our house, or who this Santa is who's coming over, but I have to admit, I am caught up in Zoë's enthusiasm.

The day comes for us to find the perfect tree. Denny helps Zoë put on her waffle stompers and her puffy jacket.

"It might be cold up at the tree farm," he says. "And the weather report said there could be snow."

"Snow!" Zoë cheers. "I love snow! It feels like Christmas!"

I've seen snow in pictures, but I don't know what it feels like.

We drive across the lake on the floating bridge, which I always enjoy because I am part water dog on my mother's side. Then we drive a long time on a fast highway. We get off the highway in a small town with old shops.

When we get to the Christmas tree farm, Zoë asks, "Can we go to the barn first?"

"Sure!" Denny replies.

And what a wonderful barn it is! It's big and warm
and smells *so* good.
A giant tree stands in the middle of the room,
glittering with lights and ornaments.

"The cookies are over here," Zoë whispers to me.
We find the cookies, and Zoë gives me one. It's very good!
"Let's find our tree," Denny says.
"Our *perfect* tree," Zoë corrects him.

Outside, a young person with a red hat hands Denny a saw. "The noble firs and Douglas firs are over there," he says. "The Scotch pines are that way. But if you ask me, go over the bridge, walk down a ways, and you'll see a nice patch of trees. It's farther out, so people don't usually go there. I bet you'll find your perfect tree down there."

"Are you one of Santa's helpers?" Zoë asks him.

"Sort of," he says.

"You're very tall for an elf," she observes.

"Yes," he agrees. "I am a very tall elf."

He doesn't look like any of the elves I've seen on television.

But I don't want to disappoint Zoë, so I don't say anything.

As we walk toward the bridge, we notice a group of large dogs. They're *so* big that they look like bears in dog suits!

"We're the Newfoundland Club of Seattle," a man with a bright vest tells us. "We find homes for dogs who don't have families. Our Newfies will haul your tree after you cut it down."

"How can a dog carry a whole tree?" Zoë asks.

"They pull them on the wagons," the man says. "Newfies are very strong. They are also protective, loyal, and smart, too."

"Enzo's smart," Zoë says, hugging me. I puff out my chest.

"But next to them, you *do* look kind of shrimpy," she whispers in my ear.

The man laughs, but Zoë's right. Next to the Newfies, I look a little like a shrimp.

We cross the bridge. I enjoy the cold air and the breeze, and I feel a snowflake hit my nose.

"I'm concerned about this weather," Denny says. "Let's try to find our tree quickly."

"It has to be perfect," Zoë says.

Denny stops at the nearest tree.

"How about this one?" he asks. "This looks like
a good tree to me. Nearly perfect."

But Zoë shakes her head. "It may be perfect for
someone," she says. "But not for us."

She turns and walks away. We follow.

It's snowing harder and harder. I like how it feels—the frozen air that melts when it touches my nose. The snow is sticking to the ground, too. I run around, pushing my snout in the snow and making a pile I can roll in. I decide that in my next lifetime, I will be a sled dog and mush across the Alaskan tundra!

Denny and Zoë keep looking for the perfect tree.

"This one?"
"Too scraggly."

"This one?"
"Too wide."

"This one?"
"Too bushy."

It's snowing *really* hard now.
Zoë starts playing with me in the
snowdrifts. We chase, tumble, and
roll around together.

"Look, Enzo, I made a snow
angel!" says Zoë.
I try too.

We're having *so* much fun, we almost don't
hear Denny calling.

"Come on, you two!" he says.

We turn to see Denny wave at us as he heads
off through the trees.

I roll over to get up, but the snow is slippery and I stumble face-
first into my snow angel, which looks more like a snow bat anyway.
Zoë helps me to my feet, and then we run after Denny.

We see him up ahead, so we run faster as he ducks behind a
tree. Finally we reach him.

"This one?" Denny asks, standing before a Christmas tree.

He turns to look at us. He's wearing Denny's jacket and jeans, and he's carrying Denny's saw, but he isn't Denny! He's someone else!

"I'm sorry, little girl," the man who looks like Denny says to Zoë. "I thought you were my daughter."

"I thought you were my dad," Zoë says.

"Oh!"

Just then, a little girl—wearing a jacket like Zoë's—steps out from behind a tree.

"Oh, there you are," the man says.

He turns back to Zoë.

"Can I help you find your way?" he asks.

But Zoë has already started running. I run with her, because I don't want her to get lost. We have to find Denny!

Zoë zigs and zags between the trees, sometimes
stumbling in the snow.

"Daddy!" she calls out as she runs. "Daddy!"

She's afraid of the woods, and afraid of the darkness,
which is falling quickly.

Doggedly, I follow her as we weave through the maze
of trees.

Finally, Zoë realizes that running is getting us more lost.

She sits in the snow next to a tree and cries.

"Enzo, I'm afraid," she says.

I want to tell her things aren't as bad as they seem.
People from the barn are probably looking for us right now!

I want to tell her: You can never outrun your fear; it's
faster than you.

You must *face* your fear if you hope to defeat it.

But I am a dog, so I have
no words I can use to tell her these things.
Zoë squeezes me tightly, until I can
hardly breathe.
I will do whatever I can to protect her
and make her safe.
I am a dog, and while I can't speak,
I can use the tools of my dogness. . . .

I wriggle free of Zoë and fill my lungs with air.
I let out a long howl, the cry of my brothers and
sisters—the Newfoundland dogs, those who are known for
their giant size, their strength, their intelligence. I howl!

In the distance, a Newfie howls back.
I call again.
The Newfie again responds, this time from closer by.
My brothers and sisters have heard me. And then we
hear galloping paws. And then we hear running feet.

A Newfie bursts through the trees and unleashes a massive woof.
She has a wagon tethered to her strong shoulders.
A man in a vest is with her, and he sighs with relief.
"Over here!" he calls out.

In a moment, Denny emerges through the trees. His face is red and he's out of breath.

"Zoë!" he cries.

Denny runs to Zoë and scoops her up in an embrace.

"I'm so happy I found you!" he says.

"I'm sorry I got lost, Daddy."

"Sometimes kids get lost," he says. "But dads will never stop looking for them—always know that."

Denny helps Zoë climb into the wagon; he puts a blanket over her
to keep her warm. He reaches down and pats my shoulder firmly three
times before he shakes the hand of the Newfie handler.

"Thank you for finding my daughter," Denny says.

"It wasn't me," the handler says. "My dog, Stella, and your dog . . ."

"Enzo," Denny says.

"Stella and Enzo talked to each other. They did all the work!"

I go to the big Newfie and I place my muzzle next to hers, which is a sign of respect and gratitude among dogs. She accepts my thanks with great dignity.

"We still haven't found our tree," Zoë says sadly.

"I think we'd better head home and look for our perfect tree next week," Denny says.

Zoë hangs her head, and I want to do something to help her. I look around at the beautiful woods with the snow falling on the trees, and I feel in my heart that the perfect tree is near.

And then I realize . . . Zoë has already found it!

I lean back on my haunches and howl to the sky so that everyone will know!

"What is it, Enzo?" Denny asks me.

I run over to the tree—the one Zoë stopped next to when we were afraid. The tree must have found *her*!

"Look!" Zoë exclaims. "It's the perfect tree!"
I bark twice.
"Well, I'll be," Denny says. "That's just about
the most perfect tree I've ever seen."

While the very tall elves tie our perfect Christmas tree to the car roof, I see that we're parked next to the father who looks like Denny and the girl who looks like Zoë. They have a tree on their roof, too. Denny and the other dad look at each other and laugh.

"You've got a good dog there," the other dad says. "The way he protected your daughter like that."

"Are you kidding," Denny says, scratching the spot behind my ear that I like so much. "We've got the best dog!"

Sometimes I wonder how it's possible for me to feel so much love for Denny and Zoë, but I do.

Later that night, when the tree is decorated and the house is warm, I finally understand what Christmas is. Christmas is trees that are perfect for us, and sparkly lights, and presents on the floor. But mostly, Christmas is family. For me, Christmas is Zoë and Denny. I bark to tell them what I've learned.

"Yes, Enzo," Denny says with a smile. "We know exactly what you mean."